MARISABINA RUSSO

Come Back, Hannah!

Greenwillow Books
An Imprint of HarperCollinsPublishers

For Jane Pollak

Come Back, Hannah!
Copyright © 2001
by Marisabina Russo Stark
All rights reserved.
Printed in Hong Kong by South China
Printing Company (1988) Ltd.
www.harperchildrens.com

Gouache paints were used to
prepare the full-color art.
The text type is Gill Sans.

Library of Congress
Cataloging-in-Publication Data

Russo, Marisabina.
Come back, Hannah! /
by Marisabina Russo.
    p.   cm.
"Greenwillow Books."
Summary: Fast-crawling Hannah
keeps Mama busy by getting
into all kinds of mischief around
the house.
ISBN 0-688-17383-7 (trade).
ISBN 0-688-17384-5 (lib. bdg.)
[1. Babies—Fiction. 2. Mother
and child—Fiction.] I. Title.
PZ7.R9192 Co 2001
[E]—dc21   00-034133

10 9 8 7 6 5 4 3 2 1
First Edition

Hannah likes to crawl across the rug, across the floor, and sometimes even up the stairs.

"Come back, Hannah!"

Mama scoops up Hannah and says,
"Please stay near me while I finish
writing this letter."

Hannah plays with her blocks. Hannah rolls her ball. There goes the ball out the door, into the hall.

album

"Come back, Hannah!"

Hannah crawls faster and faster until Mama catches her. "You are faster than a crab on the beach," says Mama. "Now you sit here next to me on the floor while I do my exercises."

Hannah watches Mama. She crawls over to the bookcase. One book, two books, more and more books, all on the floor.

When Mama sees the mess, she says, "Oh, no!"
Hannah says, "Uh-oh," and crawls away, around
a corner into the kitchen.

"Come back, Hannah!"

Hannah laughs when Mama catches her.
"You are faster than a mouse in the field,"
says Mama. "Can you sit here on this
blanket with your toys while I make one
telephone call?"

Hannah hammers the red peg, the blue
peg, and the green peg. Hannah hears
the *jingle jangle* of the dog's collar.
Where is he?

Hannah crawls right past Mama, around
the corner to Jake's bed. Jake is chewing
on a bone.

"Come back, Hannah!"

When Mama catches up, there is Hannah sitting on top of Jake.

"You are faster than a lizard on a tree!" says Mama. Mama sits down on the floor. "Please come here, Hannah," she says, patting her lap.

But Hannah crawls away, past the coffee table, past the armchair, past the books, all the way back to the kitchen, where she opens a cabinet. *Clang, clang, clang!* The pots and pans are all over the floor.

"Come back, Hannah!"

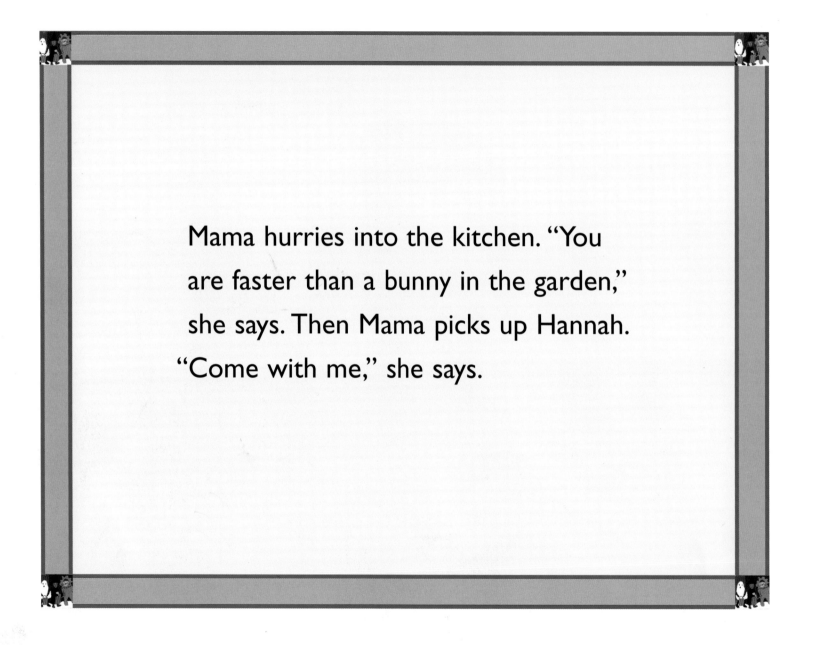

Mama hurries into the kitchen. "You
are faster than a bunny in the garden,"
she says. Then Mama picks up Hannah.
"Come with me," she says.

Mama carries Hannah back to the living room. Mama sits down on the rocking chair, and Hannah sits on her lap. "Look!" says Mama. She is holding a book. Time to read.

Hannah turns the pages. Mama reads the words. It is the story about a crab, a mouse, a lizard, and a bunny. They have a race. They have a party. Last page. The end.

"More," says Hannah.

So Mama reads the book again and again.

Then Hannah slides down off Mama's lap
and crawls across the rug as fast as she can.

"Come back, Hannah!"

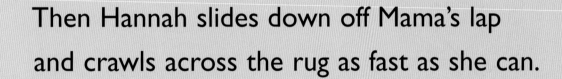

Mama hurries to catch Hannah and scoop her up in her arms. "Come here, my speedy little girl," says Mama as she kisses Hannah's cheek. "It is time for your nap."

Then Mama carries Hannah across the rug,
across the floor, and up the stairs to her room,
where her blanket and teddy are waiting.